THE TAXIDERMIED MAN

JACY MORRIS

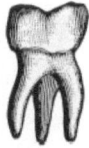

ISBN: 978-1-68510-063-6 (sc)
ISBN: 978-1-68510-064-3 (ebook)

First printing edition: October 28, 2022
Printed by Bizarro Pulp Press in the United States of America.
Cover Design and Layout: Don Noble
Edited by Nick Day
Proofreading and Interior Layout by Scarlett R. Algee

Bizarro Pulp Press, an imprint of JournalStone Publishing
3205 Sassafras Trail
Carbondale, Illinois 62901

Bizarro Pulp Press books may be ordered through booksellers or by contacting:

JournalStone | www.journalstone.com

THE TAXIDERMIED MAN

CHAPTER 1: THE TAXIDERMIST

A BUCKET OF GUTS. That's the first thing that Bud noticed when he stepped out of his rust-bucket pickup truck. The old gal used to say Datsun on the back in shiny, black letters, but the tailgate had long since been removed. Now it was a no-name, no-account wanderer like himself. One summer day, while hanging with his cousins Marco and Dusty, they had pried the tailgate free. His cousins weren't around anymore, had gone to join the elders, but the tailgate was still there, sandwiched between the banks of a particularly annoying creek that had dared keep them from reaching their favorite fishing spot.

When they were younger, and Dusty still had all of his toes (he had them amputated due to complications with diabetes), they hadn't minded getting their shoes wet from splashing through the shallow creek. Those were the one-pair-of-shoe times, and for those that only ever had one pair of shoes, you knew they were on borrowed time anyway, so you just splashed on through that muddy creek and hoped they lasted a little bit longer. But that summer, Marco had invested in a slick pair of cowboy boots. Bud didn't understand why he wanted the boots of the enemies, but it had been going around town back then. Those boots didn't stop the white people in town from busting Marco's balls, but hey, it had been worth a try.

Shaking his head, Bud straightened his mind once more. It seemed like he had to do that more and more these days. Early onset dementia had turned him into a time traveler of sorts. One minute, he would be in the middle of an errand, and the next thing he knew, he would have spent an hour standing in one spot and reliving moments that didn't really mean anything. His mind was like a hose now, coiled and tangled despite all of his best efforts. Every time he would straighten it, it would spring right back to a knotted mess. Bud had grown tired of fighting it.

The bucket of guts, with its rotten death stench, propelled him into movement. Hoping the rickety, dry-rotted porch didn't break underneath him, he mounted the crumbling steps, reached out a brown fist, and pounded on the front door. He tried to wait, tried to be patient, but before he knew it, his knuckles were bleeding, and a man was rushing for the front door with a rusted shotgun in his hand.

Bud didn't know the man personally, but he knew of the man. If you got yourself a badass trout, real wall material, and you wanted it stuffed, everyone knew that Jason Brooks was the man to go to. The beer-bellied man could take a living fish and turn it into a work of art you could stick on your wall and tell your family and friends about for years, until they got sick of it, until they could tell the fucking story as if it was their own. His cousin Marco had nabbed a twelve-point buck a few years ago, named it Pam because it had a perfect rack, and when he was drinking, he would decorate each point of that buck's stuffed head with an empty beer can, just to show everyone. He would have liked to have seen what would have happened if Marco had ever bagged another one... would he drink twenty-four beers just to show everyone how many points they had? Probably. But Marco wasn't telling stories anymore because Marco was dead.

The man inside yanked the door open. "What the fuck are you banging on my door for? You lookin' to get shot?"

Bud cleared his mind once more, straightened the hose. "I'm looking for Jason Brooks. I got a job for him."

The man, upon hearing his name, let the barrel of his shotgun drop a bit. "I'm always looking for work. But I don't stuff no poached game, just so you know. Game warden comes around here couple times a month, checking to see if I'm up to anything illegal."

"No, no, it's nothing illegal. I'm good."

"Yeah, well, whatchu want stuffed?"

"Me."

Brooks' jaw dropped for a second, and then he laughed like old Bud was trying to pull one over on him. "Get the fuck out of here! Peanut send you up here to fuck with me?" The man leaned against his screen door, looking left and right, expecting Peanut to appear at any moment.

Bud didn't say anything. The entire exchange was going about as he had expected it to.

Not seeing the mysterious Peanut, Brooks stepped back from the screen door and looked Bud up and down. "You're serious." The barrel of the shotgun came up. "You crazy or somethin'?"

Bud shook his head. He wasn't necessarily crazy, or maybe he was. All he knew was he didn't have much time before he wouldn't be able to unkink the hose. Years, maybe, but not much more. Eventually his mind would go, drift away like morning fog in sunlight. "I'm Indian."

"Pshhh, might as well be crazy then."

A vein of anger shot through Bud's thoughts, and he didn't know if it was justified or just part of his early-onset dementia. He fought his temper, reigned it in like a bucking bronco, combatted it with a smile. If he blew this, he would blow it all. "I'm not crazy. It's for religious purposes." It wasn't, but this good ol' boy would never know that.

"Religious, huh?"

"Yuh, religious."

"Like the Great Spirit or whatever? Peyote, all that bullshit?"

"Just like all that bullshit." He could see Brooks coming around, could see the wheels turning in his head as he pondered the steps needed to accomplish the task at hand.

"Did Warden Combs send you up here? He's had it in for me for years. I stole his girl—for a month anyway."

"I don't know Warden Combs. I'm here of my own free will."

Brooks scratched at his patchy, gray beard. His red-rimmed eyes squinted at Bud, but he wasn't telling him to fuck off, which was a good sign.

"Come on in," Brooks said, pushing the squealing screen door open with the barrel of his shotgun.

Inside, Brooks set the shotgun down and handed him a Silver Bullet. Bud put it into his skull as he explained his reasoning for wanting to be stuffed. He gave the man some line about his spirit and his body, how if he let his body rot, he would go on to the next world, leaving his woman behind. But he wasn't ready to leave her, not yet anyway... and that part was true. The rest of it was pure bullshit.

His life with Barb had been a charmed, wonderful thing, and sometimes, when he was cursing the fate of the disease that was tearing his mind apart, he would remember all the good times. Barb needed him, and he needed her—wanted to be with her forever, even if that meant he had to live inside his own stuffed body. Bud didn't know much about religion, didn't know much about the spirit world, but if there was a chance he could stick around and be the rock that Barb needed to continue living her life, then dammit, he was going to do whatever the hell he had to do to make it happen... better that than fading away.

When he finished his tale, some of it fake, some of it true, Jason Brooks leaned back in his ancient La-Z-Boy with the duct-taped arms, and he let out a loud burp. He tossed an empty silver tallboy on the ground and said, "I'm gonna need another. You?"

Bud nodded as he scanned Brooks' living room. Everywhere he looked, he saw tools of the man's trade. Glass eyes sat in a pile on a table. Plaster molds lay discarded on the floor amongst spools of twine, rusted knives that still looked sharp, and piles of sandpaper. The thought of those items being used on his own body sent a shiver up his spine, but he didn't care. It had to be done—for Barb.

Brooks returned, and Bud knew he had him on the hook by the gleam in his eye. The taxidermist tossed him another Silver Bullet. The top popped with a satisfying click and hiss, and he drank greedily as Brooks sagged into his recliner with a groan to mark his years on Earth.

"Truth be told, I always wanted to stuff a human, see how life-like I could make it."

"Well, now's your chance."

Brooks shook his head. "You sure it's alright?"

"Tribal religious ceremonies trump federal law. Hell, you might even be starting a trend. You do a good job, there's always red boys dyin', wantin' to be legends, wanting to be remembered."

"I could use the scratch."

"How muchya thinkin'?"

Brooks scrubbed a hand across his beard, and bits of dander and fluff flew into the air, highlighted by the sun shining through his front window. The eyes on the table gleamed and sparkled as if they were alive. But those eyes couldn't compare to the gleam in Brooks' eyes at the prospect of money.

"Well, Bud, the way I see it, this is a pretty big favor. I could get in a lot of trouble here. I'm takin' quite a risk."

Bud sensed the man mulling numbers in his mind. Cold-calculation lurked underneath those shining, greedy eyes. The taxidermist weighed Bud, totaling up his life by the truck he drove and the clothes he wore. To be honest, if he were in Brooks' position, he would probably come in at five-thousand dollars. That was the price old Marco had paid for Pam and her twelve-point rack.

"Ten thousand," Brooks shot out, hissing a little bit after he said it, instantly regretting the number.

"Done," Bud said.

Brooks half-stood, half-squatted with his hand held out, greedy to get the handshake in. As Bud stood, he left the man hanging and drained the cool beer in his hand. The can made a hollow clink as he set it on the coffee table, then he pulled a package from his back pocket. His lower back ached from sitting on it for the last hour. But that wouldn't matter for much longer.

The package spilled open as he tossed it on Brooks' janky, coffee room table. The flash of green bills caught Brooks' eyes, and he fell to his knees thumbing through the bills.

"You'll find twelve thousand in there for your trouble. There's also instructions for how I wanna be stuffed. You can keep my truck."

Brooks was too busy counting the money to pay attention as Bud pulled a revolver from his waistband, placed it under his chin, and then said, "Sorry about the mess." He squeezed the trigger... and then, nothing happened.

CHAPTER 2: HOMECOMING

BUD DIDN'T KNOW WHAT happened next. It was as if he had simply turned off for a bit, gone away. All he felt was a darkness and a cold that never seemed to end. For a while there he thought maybe the Christians were right, and he had been sent to Hell. *What'll Barb think? Will she be repulsed by him? Will she stop loving me?* It was a possibility, but he knew this was something that had to be done. He knew he wouldn't be able to force his demise upon her. He didn't want her to have to watch him fall apart, to watch his mind shrivel and fade until he was some drooling simp in a corner. He never wanted her to experience the moment when he couldn't recognize her. According to the doctors, it would happen sooner or later, and then they'd shove him in a wheelchair and toss him in one of those places where the white people kept their old people. He didn't want to go there, didn't want to be warehoused like an old couch in a storage unit.

It was better like this, like a Band-Aid ripped off in one go. He didn't know how long he was in the freezer, but it must have been long enough for old Brooksie to figure out things with the authorities and Barb. His first image, the first sign that he still had vision, came as the freezer door was thrown open. Someone slid his body into harsh fluorescent light, and then he saw Barb's face looming over his own as she had done a million times before in bed. Only this time, the kiss didn't come. Her eyes streamed with tears, and somewhere in his rotting body, he felt guilt. Then she disappeared, and he was left in the dark again, freezing and cold.

****

Brooks looked like shit. He had been drinking his way through Bud's money at an epic pace. Though Bud couldn't move and his gaze was fixed on the ceiling, every fifteen minutes or so, he heard the man pop the top of another beer and take a sloppy slurp. The man's stale beer breath wafted over him as Brooks hummed away at his work— preserving Bud's body.

Though he hadn't expected it, it was disconcerting to be stuck inside his body. His eyes were open all the time now, and he could only see that which was right in front of his face. For days, all he saw was the plain, cottage cheese ceiling of Brooks' workroom and Brooks' face as he leaned over him from time to time. Sometimes he heard voices in other parts of the house, but no one ever talked to Bud. Except for the times when Brooks worked on his body, he was completely invisible.

The worst part of the situation was that he still felt pain. As Brooks sliced open his abdomen and threw his soft parts in a bucket, hot fire lanced through him. As Brooks removed his skin inch by inch with a filet knife, electric pain knotted his mind. When the knife hovered over his eyes, Bud tried to scream, and though the first slice was the worst pain he had ever felt, he could still see, so that was something. It seemed that his senses were not tied physically to his body. For even though his skin and his nerves were gone, the pain did not disappear. Even though his eyes were removed, dangling like globs of snot in Brooks' hand, he could still see.

Eventually, he made acquaintances with the pain, became used to it; he settled into it like a bed made from broken glass. If you didn't move, it would be fine. He found that if he didn't dwell on it too much, he didn't experience the pain as intensely, but for those first few days, all he did was scream in his own mind.

Later, as he lay on Brooks' work table, he had a lot of time to reflect on his situation. Well, maybe wonder was more accurate. He pondered the ability of his consciousness to stick with the remains of his body. When Brooks pulled the remains of his brain through his nostrils, *Egyptian mummy-style* in the man's own enthusiastic words, he was sure that his consciousness would be pulled right out with him. But it wasn't. He stuck there, centralized in his skull, and he could feel a phantom version of himself. Even as his skin was removed, his insides pulled out, and his muscles and eyeballs discarded, he still felt his entire body as if it were still there. It was a strange sensation, painful and excruciating. But when one could do nothing about their pain, eventually one just gave in. Though he didn't know how long he would be trapped in his body, if he could be with Barb, it would all be worth it.

Time was different now, or possibly, he was losing time. Maybe his hose was still kinked. Perhaps the degenerative condition of his mind was more a malady of the soul than of his actual physical brain. Though there were times when all he did was stare at the ceiling for hours on end, he still found himself disappearing into the past, as if he had stepped through a portal and directly into his memories. One minute, he'd be staring at the ceiling, and the next, Bud would find himself working in the battery factory again, stapling nickel strips to the end of batteries with a spot weld machine. For hours it seemed, he would toil there, placing two batteries on the platform, lowering the electrodes using a black-handled wheel, and listening to the small beep as the electrodes fused the aluminum strip to the batteries. He would toss the finished battery pack in a red plastic tray, and so on and so forth for hours on end. In his mind, it seemed like he was actually there. He tried to control these times, to do anything different, but he was just as helpless in these memories as he was in real life. Day after day, he spent time in the battery factory, when what he really wanted to do was relive memories of his life with Barb. *Where was she? Had she forgotten about him? Abandoned him?*

During one of these moments, he was interrupted by something happening in the real world, and the battery plant around him dissolved like Styrofoam in gasoline. He felt the sensation of movement, as if his entire body were floating. It was a strange sensation to move without trying, especially since, as far as he could tell, he was upright. The world had gone white, obscured behind a cotton sheet.

The movement stopped, and he waited and waited for someone to pull the sheet from his head so he could see where he was, but it didn't happen. A door closed gently, and then silence assaulted him. *Where can I be? Did Brooks just throw me away? Did he put me in an ad in the classifieds? How much did I go for?* Bud wouldn't put it past that son of a bitch. His understanding of Brooks had grown over however long he had been trapped in his workshop. The man was a porn addict, a real pervert, and spent long hours grunting and groaning out of sight of Bud, though sometimes he was in the same room. That was all Bud needed to know about the man. How he could tug the gentleman with a dead body in the room was beyond him, but he wasn't actually surprised. A man that worked recreating life from rotting bodies... well, it was a weird vocation. Like Norman Bates and his stuffed birds. As soon as that poor Janet Leigh saw those stuffed animals, she should have known to get the hell out of that motel.

Bud was replaying what he remembered of the film through his mind when his world was suddenly turned upside down. The white sheet was ripped from his body, and there stood his Barb. Dark circles ringed her eyes, as she stood staring at him. Her face looked long and wrinkled, as if his death had tacked on five years' worth of age. He tried to smile at her, but his body, now more plaster than original Bud, no longer worked like that.

His love stared at him, pain glistening in her eyes. He soaked in the sight of her. Though she was sad, and she was probably furious at what he had done, he was sure that...

Everything went white again. It would be a long time before he saw Barb once more.

****

Along with a stack of hundred-dollar bills, he had left specific instructions for Brooks regarding the construction of his new body. He wanted the body to last, didn't want his skin to dry out and look like some sort of crazy Indian mummy. Bud had gifted Brooks with a recipe for plasticizing his skin, creating a cellular mold that, when covered with a clear-coat of epoxy, would leave him looking as life-like as possible. In addition, Bud had told Brooks to reinforce certain areas of his body. His hips and his chest should be structurally reinforced to the point where another body could... sit upon him. In addition, he had left instructions on how to keep Bud's ship sailing. If Brooks had done his job right, he would be a fully functional, even if immobile, sex partner.

He knew it was weird, somewhat strange, but Barb had always been a shy sort. Once he was gone, he didn't know that she would ever find someone else to love her, and Bud had found this infinitely sad, more so than his own death even. Above all else, Barb deserved to be happy. Before he had killed himself, he had often bemoaned the fact that Barb hadn't thrown in her lot with someone a little more durable.

She deserved the very best, and Bud hadn't been it. He had known it for the longest of times. But he had been greedy, sure that somewhere down the line he would transform into an actual good person. But that plan had always been inextricably linked with tomorrow, and as everyone knows, tomorrow never comes. It was always today, baby, and he had remained a piece of shit for all of his life, crashing on his friend's couches when he got too drunk to drive home, flying into rages that would frighten the hell out of Barb, losing his jobs, which were infrequent and far between because he'd occasionally show up to work drunk.

When Barb removed the sheet for the second time, he found himself staring up at the ceiling. He recognized the ceiling fan above. Dust peeked over the edge of the immobile fan blades, and it looked like it hadn't been cleaned in some time. Then he felt something... down there.

The top of Barb's head bobbed into his vision. She was on him, riding him. Barb's moans had a frantic, needy edge to them, and he felt it in the energy she used to fuck him. Her groans came fast, and her hands pressed against his reinforced chest cavity as time melted away. He was back, with Barb, and she was loving him.

The pleasure and the ecstasy almost drowned out the pain of his missing body parts. For the first time since he had painted Brooks' ceiling with his brains, he actually felt good, and then it all melted away. Barb's groans changed suddenly, shifting from ecstatic moans to a less enthusiastic grunt, and then her pelvis stopped moving. She slid off of him, and somewhere in the room, she sobbed. "Fuck you, Bud, you selfish son of a bitch. I hate you," she cry-spoke. Though he couldn't turn to look at her, he could imagine that look on her face. Barb's cry face was hideous and painful to behold, and even when he was a fifth-deep, that face always shocked him sober, even if it was just for a few minutes. It was the type of face that one would do anything to make go away. He was ashamed to admit that he had been the cause of that face far too often.

Barb's grief-stricken visage flashed in his vision for a moment before she threw the sheet over his body once more. That was the last time he saw Barb.

****

"What is that?" a man's voice asked.

"I know it's weird, but it's the body of my dead husband."

"What? You've gotta be fucking kidding me!"

"I know. I know. I just can't bear to part with it."

"That's sick... can I see it."

"He's not some sideshow freak to gawk at."

"Listen, I'm not sure what you're into, but this is all a little weird for me."

"No, don't go. It's ok. I didn't have him made. My husband was losing his mind, and he killed himself and paid someone to stuff his body."

"Why don't you bury him?"

"It was his last wish."

"Ugh. It gives me the fucking creeps."

Bud listened to a brief kissing exchange, fury growing in his chest. He tried to ball his non-responsive hands into fists, but they wouldn't move. He felt his non-existent heart break.

The kissing ceased, and the unseen man said, "I can't. Not with him in here."

"Ok."

Bud tried to grit his teeth. His consciousness rattled in his prison, shaking the bars, for he knew now that's what it was. From the other room, he heard the groans of his wife, and he swore up and down, left and right, even fucking diagonal, but there was nothing he could do about it.

Over time, he saw how stupid he had been, assuming Barb was nothing without him. It had always been the other way around. She didn't have any friends because he didn't want her to have any friends. No one ever hit on her, because he was known for knocking out the teeth of anyone that looked at his wife the wrong way. He had assumed she felt the same way about him, but he knew now he had been lying to himself. Maybe it had been the dementia, or maybe he had always been a blind fool.

Over time, Barb's voice grew old and croaked with age. Somehow, the man stayed around, and sometimes he heard them talking in other rooms, sometimes arguing, sometimes loving each other.

****

If he could have blinked, he would have. But his eyelids were glued into place. If he could have seen himself in the mirror, Bud would have pegged the look on his face as one of surprise.

The man in front of him was old, somewhat shorter than Bud had been. Gently he had lowered the sheet from Bud's head. His eyes held a bit of curiosity, and his breath reeked of cheap whiskey, not the good shit. Even after all these years, Bud could tell the difference. After all, he had enjoyed his fair share. Actually, he had enjoyed the fair shares of a small village. His doctor, a cold bastard who had no love for Indians, once said, "If your mind don't get you, your fucking liver will."

The man with the old face sneered at him. "So this is the great Bud?" He swayed from side to side, and when he spoke, he oozed the words out, sluggish and slow. "You're a freak, Buddy boy. An absolute freak." He fell silent again, his body tottering in the familiar sway of the inebriated. Bud had seen that dance a million times in the mirror before. "Let's see what you're working with down there." The man yanked the sheet from Bud. A cloud of dust filled the air, and the man rocked back on his heels. He smiled and took another drink from the highball glass, the lone ice cube clinking against its sides. "Looks like I'm an upgrade." He tossed the sheet haphazardly over Bud's body, and through the wrinkled fabric, he heard the heavy footsteps of the man as he walked away.

An upgrade. Fuck you, Buster. No one had told him that's what the man's name was, but that's what he decided to call him. He looked like an old-washed up detective from a black and white movie. Spoke like it too. Bud hated the man. How could Barb take up with him? Later that night, he heard more of their loud sex, and he tried to remember if Barb had ever groaned for him like that. He decided she hadn't. If he hadn't already done it, he would have killed himself again.

****

Throughout the house, heavy footsteps pounded on the floor above. It had been a long time since anyone had visited him: a long, lonely time. The last visit he had was when someone had silently moved him to a quiet place in the house. He didn't know how much his taxidermied body weighed, but he was light enough to be carried by a single man. Based upon the bouncing and jouncing, he had been moved down to the basement, a dusty hole that no one ever visited.

"So the whole lot? There's nothing you want to keep?" a voice asked.

"Nothing," Buster said. Bud recognized his voice by its gravely timbre. "There's too many memories here. I just want a clean break. Now that my wife's gone, I gotta get out of here. But, I figured since you were nice enough to take everything off my hands, I oughta do you the favor you of showing you this. Wouldn't want you thinking I killed someone. Hell, that's what I'd think if I was in your position."

The sheet snapped as Buster yanked it from his body. The cold, damp air of the basement kissed his plasticized skin.

"Jesus, it's hideous!" a wormy, white man said.

"Tell me about it. It's my late wife's first husband. Bastard shot himself and had his body stuffed. I read the note. He was one sick puppy, but Barb couldn't ever part with him. Gave us the fucking creeps, but he had no family, so she sorta felt responsible for it."

"What the fuck am I supposed to do with it?"

"I don't know. Light it on fire. Give it away, float it down the goddamn Rogue River for all I care."

The man stepped in front of Buster and shined a flashlight up and down Bud's body. The light stung Bud's eyes, and he felt fear for the first time in a long time, probably since he had actually been alive. *What's he gonna do with me?*

Bud wondered if his soul still knew how to fly. Maybe if the man lit him on fire, he would be freed from his prison. Maybe he could find Barb in the afterlife. Maybe she might even want to see him, though judging by the wrinkles on Buster's face and the bald pate of his livers-potted head, it had been decades since she had even bothered looking at him. And now she was dead, gone onto whatever came next without him, and he was stuck here. He was a sucker.

"What are you gonna do with it?" Buster asked.

"Beats me. But I'll figure something out. He looks Indian."

"Correctamundo."

"Hmm... that might be a problem. You know how they are about their remains."

"Nope. And I don't care. You want all our shit, then this guy goes with. It's your problem now."

The man stung Bud's eyes again with the flashlight.

"Deal?" Buster asked.

The man with the flashlight turned and held his hand out. "Deal." The two men shook, and with that, Bud was evicted from his home.

CHAPTER 3: SORROW IS PURPLE AND MAKES YOU WANT TO THROW UP

FOR A WHILE, BUD'S only stimulus came from his own mind. He looked at the tapestry of his life, noting the rips and the tearstains. Barb's face came to him often, young and vibrant. When she appeared, she smiled for him, and he drank in the quirk of her lips, imagining he had said something funny. Before his body had turned against him, he had used to be funny, maybe.

Sometimes, if he was lucky, he would recall lying in bed with her, breathing in the scent of her skin. Years passed in this way, and the shroud that covered him collected dust which he could smell through the aging cloth. His world was a world of darkness, though his ever-open eyes tried to spot any signs of life. Occasionally, he heard sounds, the skittering of creatures in the darkness. Cockroaches, maybe mice, but they didn't talk to him or seem interested in him at all. He wasn't even worth a rat's curious nibble.

For all intents and purposes, he was completely forgotten, his spirit trapped in a body made of plaster, stuffing, and wooden supports. If glass eyes could weep, his cheeks would have been stained with salt deposits, a crystallized tattoo of grief.

Then, one day, that all changed. As the dusty sheet draped over his head lit up with a faint orange light, he once again experienced a sense of movement.

"Come on, Bud," a man said. The man grunted and groaned as he struggled to transport Bud's corporeal body. He relished those groans, ate them up the way he had used to wolf down nachos at the bowling alley, back when he and his cousins, long gone now, had been in a league. They had never won a damn thing, except for the occasional fistfight, but they had lived like kings, slurping down three-dollar Buds and swelling their bellies with cheap bar food.

He missed his cousins, the last two members of his family. That he should be the last one still on the earth bolstered his sadness, deepened it to a shade of purple that would make you throw up if you saw it.

"Damn this thing is heavier than it looks," another man said.

Though he couldn't speak, Bud knew that the weight most likely came from the years of sorrow collected in his soul.

"Yeah, well, it's worth its weight in gold."

As his body jostled left and right, up and down, Bud got the sense that he was being carried up and out of a basement. They hauled his body through some hallways, bumping him against the drywall. His fake body registered the pain half-heartedly. Long ago, he had come to grips with the pain of being dead. The thing about pain is, after a while, it's just the way it is, like the temperature or the weather. Ain't nothing to do about it, so you just accept it and move on.

The world brightened, and through the dusty sheet, he could smell the out-of-doors, and his mind, never fully recovered from its degeneration, whisked him away to long ago memories. His plastic skin glowed with the heat of sunshine, and he longed for the men to remove the sheet so he could see the outside world once more.

"Well, I helped you carry it. Least you can do is show it to me."

"Yeah, I guess so."

The man pulled the sheet from Bud's body gingerly, like an archeologist unwrapping a mummy. The slow reveal of the world made him ache in ways he hadn't expected. The world around him was ugly, a place of concrete and chain-link fences. It was warm out, and if his body still had the capability to sweat, it would have. Despite its grotesque appearance, he soaked it all in— the ugly industrial area, the burning sun, the faces of the two down-trodden men, with their worker's hands and trader's eyes. His eyes feasted.

"Golly. This guy's at full attention."

"Yeah. Not bad huh?" This from a skinny-headed man with thinning hair and thick eyeglasses. Though years had passed, and the man's face had become marred with the blemishes of time, this was the man that had purchased him. "Ya jealous?"

"Shoot. I mean, an average guy would be jealous, but not me."

"Get outta here," the skinny-headed man said. Then the man looked Bud in the eyes and said, "You're gonna like where you're going, pal. Shoot. Kinda wish I could trade places with you."

With that, the second man obscured his vision with bubble wrap, stealing the ugly world away. As they wrapped him, his ears drank in their banal conversation, devouring every syllable, every sound, and savoring it like a child who has their Halloween candy doled out to them one piece at a time. When they were done, they picked him up and placed him on his back. Memories of the last time he had been on his back assaulted him. *Barb...* They showered him with packing peanuts, and he sobbed in his mind as they hammered the lid of the crate shut.

Compared to the years he had spent in the basement of wherever the trader had stored him, the trip wasn't long. Bud quite enjoyed the rocking movement as he was transported to his mysterious destination. It reminded him of his childhood, when the world's rules hadn't been so strict. He remembered being shorter than his dad's knee, rolling around in the back of a red hatchback, the kind everyone seemed to own in the eighties. Lying on his back on the scratchy carpet, he would look up through the hatchback's rear window and watch the world as it passed him by: light poles, electrical wires, the occasional bird, an airplane. A glorious existence, a time that could never be brought back. Always forward. Such a shame. If only he could go back in time. But still the movement was nice.

During his trip, there was only one interruption, one halt. Wooden nails squealed as someone pried open the crate. Then a voice, speaking in Spanish to an unseen partner, leaned over his body, swiped at the packing peanuts, and ripped the bubble wrap. Bud's Spanish was rusty. He hadn't been a good student, but he knew all the swearwords, and this man was going through all of them.

His eyes widened at first, and then his brown face shriveled up. *Is my body aging that poorly? Surely, the man has seen bodies before.* Clad in a Mexican customs officer uniform, the man reached out and poked his skin. Bud roiled at the sensation of actual human contact, for however briefly. The man recoiled and spat out a few of the words that Bud knew, and then he threw the bubble wrap and packing peanuts back over his face. After the concussive sound of a nail gun sealing up his crate, his journey continued.

****

When next he was unpacked from the crate, his senses were assaulted by the reek of cigar smoke, sweat, and stale beer. The place he found himself was dingy. A layer of dust clung to the ceiling. Someone ripped the bubble wrap from his face, and he was lifted unceremoniously upright. The wide, brown eyes of a shiny faced man greeted him. His skin glowed brown in the rough light. Not like the brown skin of his father or mother, but polished, glossier. The man's teeth were brown too, and the stub of a cigar poked out between them.

The man smiled at him like a child on Christmas morning, and then said something in Spanish that Bud didn't understand. A puff of cigar smoke wreathed Bud's head as the man turned and presented him to a group of haggard, brown-skinned women. Despite the joy on the man's face, the women on the couch didn't look particularly enthused, and Bud wished he had paid more attention in Spanish class. But how could he with Marla Thibodeaux sitting there, looking the way she had?

One of the women stood, her ponderous breasts jiggling with every high-heeled step she took across the stained black and white linoleum. All he could see was the top of her head and her eyes as she stared him in the face. The skin under her eyes was pouched and baggy, and it looked like she hadn't slept in some time. She reeked of strong perfume, and then he felt her hand on his gear.

Sorry, Barb. This had never been part of his plan, and he felt guilt as the woman stroked his stuffed manhood. The woman laughed a shrill, stark laugh, and the other women laughed along with her. Then they left him alone, and he soaked in his new home. It was a small bar, dark and empty. Janky tables sat propped level with flattened beer cans, ready to topple over at a moment's notice.

The women in the room bustled about, busying themselves with preparations for the day. The more haggard women cleaned half-assedly, sweeping dirt from one corner to another. The girls that still held onto a modicum of their youth prepared as well, sitting at the bar in their skimpy outfits, while a square-headed bartender with black hair continually filled their drinks.

Mexico. This has to be Mexico. Other than movies, he had never been down south, but this was exactly what he had imagined in his mind, only seedier—and sadder. The smiling man with the greasy, shiny face wheeled him backward down a dark, dank hallway and into a room that smelled of unwashed sex sheets. He laid Bud on his back, and he was forced to stare up at a mirrored ceiling covered in handprints.

For a while, he lay like this, wondering what was going to happen next. He had some sort of inkling, and he spent his time apologizing to Barb. If her spirit roamed free, he expected her to slap the shit out of him at any moment.

As he muttered his thousandth apology for what was to come, the thump of music rocked the flimsy walls. In between apologies, he studied his own nightmarish face. Brooks was a shit taxidermist, and he had come out looking like some sort of Neanderthal. From other rooms, he heard the sounds of coupling, frantic and exaggerated. Women called out to *Dios*; he knew that one. Men did the same in grunting, slurred voices thick with alcohol and other substances.

Maybe they forgot about me. Bud readied himself for the possibility he would be stuck lying on this bed staring at his reflection in a mirror for the rest of his afterlife, and then he heard the door to his room squeal open. A switch clicked, and a red light came on. Red lights were good; they hid all sorts of nasty blemishes and sores that could kill the mood. In the mirror, his face didn't look so botched when bathed in crimson. A crowd of drunken English voices, slurred and overly-excited, entered the room.

"What the fuck is this?" a man with a heavy country twang asked.

Another, more civilized voice, added, "We paid for a donkey show."

With a Spanish accent, a woman said, "This better than donkey."

"No, no, no," a third voice said. "We paid for a donkey show, and this isn't what we talked about. What even is that?"

"It's a man. He stuffed. See. He's long." He felt an overly moisturized hand caress him down there, and he called Barb's name once more in apology.

"Fuck it!" the man with the country twang said, his voice thick with alcohol. "I'll be the donkey."

"No, no, no," the civilized voice said. "We're out of here."

Apparently, what the civilized man said went for the entire group. Footsteps receded from the room, and he thought he was alone.

"I'll watch," an as yet unheard voice said.

"You watch. I ride good. You have money?"

The rest of the exchange went down quickly, and Bud was forced to watch in the mirror as the prostitute mounted him. A voice off to the side shouted encouragement, and he heard the revolting sound of a zipper, followed by the even more revolting *chucka-chuk* of a man pleasuring himself to the sights and sounds of an ancient hooker riding a stuffed body.

What have I done? Who am I? Barb is going to kill me. But he was already dead. Now, all that was left was for his soul to catch up to his body.

He imagined what his cousin Marco would have done in this position. Hell, if Marco knew how this was going to be, this was definitely how he would have chosen to go out. He might have had himself stuffed when he was twenty. It would have been a happier ending for Marco, literally.

Can a soul catch an STD? He wished he could Google the answer, not because he expected to find it, but because he thought the answers might be funny, and he could use a laugh right about now.

Moisture dripped down his hips, and he knew the prostitute wasn't faking it anymore. Her slippery hands slid against the tight, hard skin of his chest, and he tried not to respond to the sensation. But, he had to admit, it felt good... and well, he didn't have a choice.

Her saggy breasts jiggled tantalizingly in his face, and the slap of her thighs against his plasticized pelvis rang throughout the small room. She screamed in ecstasy, and then she lay on his body, pressing the softness of her breasts into his skin. After she dismounted, Bud cried inside his hollow shell.

Even though he hadn't seen Barb in decades, guilt gnawed at him. *I enjoyed it! I cheated! I'm the worst person that ever lived, and I'm not even alive!*

The light in the room clicked off, and he listened to the sounds of coitus coming from other rooms, but no one visited him again that night.

****

But the visits didn't stop. They continued, and over time, Bud became desensitized to the whole operation, to the sounds, the smells, the lustful Americans and their foul commands. He tried to not be there, tried not to indulge the experiences foisted upon him, and after a while, he stopped longing for release from his shell. As time passed, and his own self-loathing grew, he began to think he didn't deserve to go free. His spirit belonged locked here on earth. Wherever Barb was, if she was out there in the afterlife, he didn't deserve to see her.

But that was ok now. He had someone else, someone who loved him. In the early morning hours, she came to him. When the bordello fell silent and the thumping music stopped, she would slip into his room, her head down, heavy with shame. Whenever he heard her clothing rasp against her skin as she disrobed, he would know it was her. On bare feet, she would come to see him, climbing into bed and draping an arm across his chest. Bud didn't know why she cried or what sort of trauma she had experienced that would drive her to lie with a taxidermied body, but he wished he could ask. In hushed, furtive whispers, she talked to him, her hot breath condensing in the folds of his ear.

With tears in her eyes, she would kiss him. Occasionally, she would do other more carnal things to him when she was angry. His heart ached for the damaged woman, and though he had hated her at first, he came to pity her. She suffered, and his body offered her something she needed, or at least, this is what he theorized based solely upon his weak grasp of the Spanish language. He gave her unconditional love, and eventually, he felt good about it.

The woman needed it. Her eyes were puffy and bruised. The track marks on her arms told him everything he needed to know. She was trapped, and the only time she was free was when she was running a hand across his smooth chest.

"Te amo," she said as she ran an over-moisturized hand across his cheek. "Como se llama, mi amor?"

Bud.

He longed to help the woman, to help her free herself, but there was nothing he could do. Over time, her body changed. Her skin, once filled with shine and tight to her meat, began to sag. Her eyes, once full of life and a glimmer of happiness, became the eyes of a dead woman, dull and lusterless. Her teeth, once large and white, turned brown, and then began to disappear altogether.

One night, she stumbled into his room, barely able to walk. By the reflection of the mirror, he watched her stalk across the vomit and semen-stained shag carpet. Though he couldn't see her face, he recognized her from the top of her head. Her hair had begun to fall out, and he could see patches of scalp that she couldn't cover—or maybe she didn't care to cover the patches any longer.

His new love sat on the edge of the bed and opened her wrists with a dull knife.

No! No! No! Bud called to her, though he didn't know her name.

The blood came out thick and red, and then she reclined on the bed, running her withered hand across his smooth chest. Occasionally, the palm of her hand, sticky with her own life, would stick to his skin. The blood was hot at first, and then it cooled.

"Mi amor, mi amor, mi amor," she repeated over and over. And she fell into a deep sleep. Then she was gone, the second love of his life, and he hadn't even known her name.

No one came to the room for several days, and when the shiny faced man with the wide brown eyes appeared, he cussed up a storm and ran from the room. The smell was bad now.

When the paramedics arrived to remove his love, her hand came away with a ripping sound, the dried blood sticking to his chest.

Through the mirror, he saw a red-brown handprint left behind on his skin like a tattoo.

Once she was gone, wheeled out on a gurney by people who didn't seem to care about Bud's loss of love, the paramedics tried to move Bud's body as well. Hope swelled in his hollow chest for the briefest of moments, and then the man with the shiny face told them to leave him where he was. After he produced a receipt from a backroom, the revolted paramedics left. Bud wouldn't be going anywhere. Not for a while. They closed the door and turned out the lights, and he never saw his love again.

CHAPTER 4: TIME TRAVEL AND ROID BOYS

IN THE CORNER OF the shittiest bar in Juarez, Mexico, Bud stood looking out over the crumbling space. After his lover's suicide, no one came to see him, and he had been turned into décor in the bar. Over the years, he had learned a fair amount of Spanish. Sometimes, he wished he could speak, just to see how well he would be understood.

Time passed like a millipede crawling across a desert. The majority of his time he spent trying to imagine the faces of his two loves. He spent even more time apologizing to them, though he had no way of knowing if they could hear him wherever they were.

Before him, a ribald play repeated itself, the backdrop to his thoughts. The bar was a record with a scratch in it, only this time the repeated fragment lasted for twenty-four hours instead of a few seconds. People came in. Whores paraded about, trying to convince the tourists to pick them, despite their haggard faces and the track marks on their arms. The man with the shiny face supplied his patrons with drugs, beer, and tequila and anything else their sick little minds could think of. The women came and went, as did the customers, but the man with the shiny face was always there. His hair thinned, and his belly grew outward, straining his belt until he had to buy a brand new one. His fashion changed as well. He went from wearing fancy, stylish suits to more restrained button-up, collared shirts.

The fashion of the whores and customers changed as well. He didn't know how it was possible, but the whores' outfits became even more scandalous. The customers came into the club in t-shirts and shorts rather than respectable slacks. Sometimes, he would even see a dirtball American come in wearing sweatpants, their bulging erections already pulsing as they walked through the door. The man with the shiny face didn't care. The women in his employ were older, strung out on drugs, and were mostly just pink meat for the man to peddle. With only a passing interest, shiny face would watch them smoke and shoot up before the doors opened. Sometimes, when he was angry, which seemed to happen more frequently as time dragged on, he would punch them in the places that men didn't care about.

At three in the afternoon, the doors would open, and tourists, horny and three-sheets to the wind would stumble in. They would sit in the corners and watch the girls dance and parade around the room, drinking their fill until their courage and their flesh was up. Then the man with the shiny face would come over, throw an arm over their shoulder as if they were long lost friends, and they would set about haggling over the price of the girl who had caught the tourist's eye. This would go on for hours.

Loud music thumped in the small bordello, and over the years the music changed. No one ever said the names of the songs. He just noticed that over time, the trends became different... not better or worse, just different. But when an old song would come on, something that happened with increasing rarity, he would be transported away to a different time and place, whisked away by his memories. And this is how he would pass his time.

Sometime in the morning, everyone would drag their ass out of the bar, sore and hungover. An elderly man with a hangdog expression on his face would appear around ten in the morning and do a half-assed job of cleaning. Sometimes he mopped. Sometimes he didn't. On more than a few occasions, the man would walk behind the bar and get drunk for a couple of hours after he emptied all of the ashtrays and garbage.

Bud liked those times the best. As the man sat on his stool, alone in a bordello, he would drink his tiny shots of tequila and howl at the ceiling, singing in Spanish so poorly Bud couldn't help but love the sound of it.

When the man finished his work, he would leave, and Bud would be alone with his own memories for a few hours. These thoughts would invariably travel the same track as all of his thoughts. He had nothing new to think about. No one talked to him, no one engaged him in conversation, and loneliness gnawed at him like a dog with a bone. He longed for someone to leave him lying in the street so a garbage truck or a semi could come along and flatten the shit out of his taxidermied body. He was quite sure that his spirit would be free then, released from his self-imposed tomb.

But no one ever did this. Sometimes, he would try and recall every moment of his life from the time of his first memory to the present. But that got old. Eventually his mind would wander, and he would lose his place in time. Time was funny like that, shifting underneath you like quicksand at any given opportunity. Fucking time—it was all he had. If he had a wallet, and he pulled it out, a bunch of time would fall out and pool on the floor.

When the athletes came in, he was busy cursing time for the millionth time. He could tell they were athletes because they wore the same jerseys. They wore jerseys like none that Bud had ever seen, bright red and plastered in so many advertisements and logos he had no idea what the team's name was. He had only been a passing sports fan, rooting for the local teams when they made it to the playoffs, but these guys... they were not like any athletes he had ever seen.

Huge and bursting with muscles, they strutted into the bar like they owned the place. They had the type of bodies that let you know they were going to erupt into violence at some point in the evening simply for the fact that they were bigger than everyone else. Their forearms bulged with veins and their chests were large and built like iron-bound barrels. The athletes crowed and hooted at everything, their voices rising louder and louder, as if even talking was a competition among them. Despite their bluster, nothing they said was particularly interesting.

Bud had wanted to be an athlete when he was younger, had even showed himself to be somewhat talented in the realm of baseball. But he didn't have the killer instinct. Oh, he liked hitting the ball and striking people out, but he didn't care if he won or lost. He was too easygoing, and his coach told him as much.

"You gotta develop that killer instinct, Bud! Go for the throat! If you don't do it, you can be damn sure that someone will be going for yours!"

Bud had simply shrugged his shoulders. Killer instinct, you either had it or you didn't. Years later, his coach would be run out of town. Rumor said he had gone for the throat at some point with one of his wards. All coaches were pieces of shit in one way or another. Mini-gods on a grass field. The people that survived the crucible of organized sports were frequently the dumbest, the most willing to sacrifice their identities for the glory of on-field greatness. Bud hadn't been one of those, and he was done with organized sports by middle school.

These people, though, these hulking, giant monsters, had dedicated their life to sports. It was all they knew... besides drinking and whoring. Quite a few wedding rings glittered on their thick fingers, but these meant nothing as the ones with rings seemed the most eager to get into bed with the shiny face man's whores.

As the night wore on, the athletes crowed louder, their obnoxiousness rising to epic heights. They called each other "bruh" and not a single whore could walk through the bar without one of them slapping them on the ass. They shouted obscenities and challenged each other to feats of strength like animals in a nature documentary, trying to prove their prowess for the women. They were brainless animals.

At one point in the night, the shiny face man produced a silver briefcase with locks like none that Bud had ever seen. He placed a thumb on a black box and the latches clicked open. Inside, he could see the gleam of tiny glass vials. With a palsied brown hand, he produced one of the vials and gave a speech to the athletes that was lost among the thumping music and the fake moans of orgasmic pleasure from the back rooms.

Then, the athletes did the oddest of things. They lined up and pulled their pants down, and the shiny face man injected them in their ass. The athletes laughed and shook their fists in the air before giving each other high fives.

They continued like this for hours, snorting cocaine off the dirty bar, disappearing into the back rooms, and drinking to the point that they all became rather violent. Fistfights broke out, and the whores looked around them with dinner plate eyes. Even the shiny face man's eyes were wide and fearful.

One of the athletes, a square, blocky man, stalked in the direction of Bud. His acne-filled face disappeared, and then suddenly, Bud was flying—no, he was being carried.

The man set him in the middle of the room, and the athletes screamed and hooted, beating their chests like gorillas.

"Get one of them whores on this dick!" the man yelled, bossing around the shiny face man.

The owner of the bar, not used to being spoken to in such a fashion, balked, not because he wouldn't have his whores do such a thing, but because he didn't like to be bossed around. He was in charge in this place, not the athletes. In Spanish, he spoke to one of the whores, and called the athlete a *fucking retard with balls like grapes.* The whore laughed at this, and the athlete flew into a rage.

With veins pulsing in his hot dog-colored temples, the beefy man picked up the shiny face man as if he were but an oversized teddy bear, and then threw the old man through the air. For a moment, he looked like Juarezian Superman sailing across the bar, his arms out before him as his graying black hair trailed behind him. Then, he crashed into Bud, and Bud felt pain for the first time in a long time. Sure, he still felt the dull, ever-present pain of being dead, but he had come to grips with that a long time ago. This pain was more intense, more excruciating, something he couldn't ignore.

Bud's world swam, and he realized he was lying on his back looking up at the dusty ceiling. The pain came from the middle of his prison and with his consciousness, he probed the pain, trying to determine what exactly had happened.

My penis! My penis is gone!

Bud panicked. He had lost his manhood. He would never love again. He watched as the shiny face man pushed off his chest, an object in his hand.

That's my dick!

The owner of the bordello disappeared from sight. Bud yearned to see, yearned to know what was going on in the rest of the bar. *What's that man doing with my dick?* Despite the pain, this was the most excitement he had experienced in years, and he couldn't see a damn thing. Then, Bud became aware of something extraordinary.

For a lack of a better word, he felt a draft where his piece had been. His mind bubbled, rising and falling like a ball of wax inside a lava lamp. Bundling himself into as tight a ball as possible, he was somehow able to disappear into the shell of his body. He journeyed through the blackness of his chest, past the wooden framework, past the exposed grid of plaster innards and toward a small pool of light. Through the hole in his groin, he was able to push his way into the outside world.

I'm free!

But he wasn't. With his mind outside of his body, he tried to float up and away, but something held him back. Something anchored him to his body. The disappointment was fleeting, however, as he realized that he could now change his perspective on the world. He could now look around.

While he would rather be untethered from his body altogether, he was still elated to be able to watch the mayhem in the bar as it unfolded.

All around the bordello, violence erupted. The shiny face man swung Bud's cock like a baseball bat, bludgeoning the athletes in the head until it snapped in two. The athletes fought amongst themselves, too plastered to distinguish between friend or foe. The whores fell into two categories of behavior. They either huddled in the corners to avoid being injured, or they clonked the athletes in the head with beer bottles. With each swing, they took out their rage about their position in life on the very people that kept them down.

Bud rooted for them, silently applauding as the old whores moved about the cantina, taking shots when they could. The giant men threw each other through the air and cracked each other in the teeth with their ham hock fists.

Then the giant white man that had started it all, held out a hand to the shiny face man, bidding him to stop his assault. The athlete doubled over, his red face straining as he alternately laughed and choked. Vomit erupted from his mouth, and Bud had never seen such a vile stream, not even from his cousin Miles who had used to drink radiator fluid to get high when they were teenagers.

All around the bar, pockets of violence faltered, some in mid-swing, as the athlete spewed his entire evening's excess upon the floor. Then, everyone laughed as if it were the greatest joke in the history of man. The athletes, some bleeding from wounds, some concussed by beer bottles, clapped each other on the shoulder, lifted each other in great, back-breaking bear hugs, and patted each other on the back. The whores moved cockroach silent, slinking to positions of safety, hoping that their assaults would be forgotten and forgiven. Even the shiny face man stopped and had himself a good laugh. He held the remains of Bud's dick in his hand, showing it to the athletes, pointing and laughing. Just like that, everything seemed alright. Reality, bent and twisted for a moment, snapped back into normality, and the glory of that excess faded among the patrons.

The night was over, and everyone wound down, some with a drink, some with on-the-house blowjobs. But, as the athletes filed out the door, there was one last piece of business, one last thing that would change Bud's death forever.

The shiny face man, with his accent thick and drunken asked, "But what about this, señor?"

The athlete looked at Bud then, and he laughed. "What about it?"

"It's worthless to me now. No one wants to see a dickless man in a bordello. It's bad luck."

The athlete turned toward Bud and said, "I'll take it off your hands. How much do you want for it?"

"I paid a pretty penny for it, señor. I couldn't see letting it go for less than five hundred."

"Two hundred!"

"Three!"

"Two-fifty!"

"Sold!" the shiny face man said, and Bud never saw him again. His world turned sideways as the giant athlete tucked him under a sweat-soaked armpit and carried him out into the cool night of the godforsaken Mexican border town.

Later that night, the Portland Punk Rockers, a professional gamer team, took Bud to a tattoo parlor. Through the hole in his crotch, Bud marveled at the process, though he wasn't a huge fan of athletes scribbling their names on his dickless body.

The tattoo artist, a skinny Mexican woman with delicate hands, purple hair, and metal in her face, pulled out a small laser. On a small keyboard, she clicked a bunch of buttons, and then, in a flowery scrawl, she emblazoned the athletes' names on his body. Bud was enraptured by the blue light of the laser, enthralled with how wherever the laser touched him, a dark stain would appear. It didn't hurt, which was good, because year after year, he would undergo the same process, even though he didn't know it then.

CHAPTER 5: THE MURDERLEAGUE YEARS

BUD'S NEWFOUND FREEDOM WAS more of a gift than a curse. Time, it seemed, had been slipping him by. The world around him was different than he expected, even accounting for the growth of the world in the time that he had been in Mexico.

People bustled about the street in compact electric cars. They always held devices up to their heads. After a while, he figured out that they were all speaking on portable phones like something right out of Star Trek.

Everywhere the Murderleague players brought him, there were crowds of people, large, out of shape people with beer guts and fat baboon faces. They spoke in a manner that was simple, unrefined, and punctuated by swear words.

The athletes that toted him around were no better. They spent most of their time sitting on their phones, swiping at the screens, with the TV on in the background. In this manner, he learned about the world that had passed him by.

It turned out, that he had become the de facto trophy of a young, upstart video game league, a death sport of sorts where people competed at video games and the losers actually died. Bud couldn't conceive of a world where people would be allowed to fight to the death like ancient gladiators in Rome. It turned out there was a simple reason for the institution of the Murderleague. There were too many fucking people on the planet.

The numbers were astounding, and it was then that Bud realized, his mind had been slipping far more often than he had imagined. He tried to put together the pieces of his past, tried to figure out how long he had been in Mexico. How long had he been in his wife's house? How long had he been traveling the world with these athletes?

He pushed himself out through his crotch, spinning his consciousness left and right, only to discover that his entire body had been covered in tattoos. Even more disturbing, he had lost one of his nipples at some point. There wasn't an inch of space left on his body, at least on the parts that he could see. He tried to wrap around his body and see if the backside was tattooed as well, but his tether only went so far.

Bud retreated inside himself like a frightened hermit crab.

On the TV, a man mentioned the Fiftieth Amendment. Bud didn't know how many amendments there had been in his lifetime, but he sure as fuck knew there hadn't been fifty. Nowhere close to that number he suspected. He tried to hearken back to his time in high school, tried to remember what he had learned about the constitution from Mrs. Light. He could recall the first three or four, but not much more than that.

"The Fiftieth Amendment, established after the world population reached twenty billion, has been something of a controversial amendment."

The athlete he was with, he didn't know his name, left the room, a bulge in his pants. At least this one didn't masturbate with him in the room. They were all the same, grunting sex machines with no personality. It was like being owned by gorillas, rich gorillas swathed in everything that a human could want, with the exception of purpose.

"Despite complaints from human rights groups, it was established that the only lives worthy of the rights set forth in the Bill of Rights were American lives. This of course, paved the way for the bloodsport known as the Murderleague, a sport where gamers, and in many cases criminals, from all over the world compete in a series of deathmatches. Now the number one sport in the world, the only rule is kill or be killed."

Bud's mind shook with the implications, which weren't many for a man with a damaged consciousness trapped in a never-ending tomb made of his own flesh. He pondered the meaning of life, pondered the fact that there were now twenty billion people on the planet.

Images began to click into place. The dirty people on the streets; hungry, defeated. They never changed, never went away. Everywhere he went, there seemed to be a row of tents and poor people sitting on the curb, waiting for their lives to end. Those sad faces passed by him whenever he was loaded into a vehicle with windows. Strung out on the street, no one seemed to mind, not the homeless, not the clean-cut people that walked along in their fancy clothing.

One day, while stopped at a traffic light, he saw one of the homeless charge at one of the non-homeless, only to be repulsed by some sort of force-field. As the homeless man sat on the sidewalk, his head in his hands begging to be killed, the man in the force-field laughed and pointed his cell phone at the man. The light turned green, and the vehicle sped away, making nary a sound, as the athlete in charge of him for that day received head from some poor man.

He was disgusted by the athletes, found them repulsive in so many ways. That he should have become their trophy, their prize for competing in a league that allowed its members to murder each other for cash and prizes disgusted him.

Bud had never been a violent man. Oh, sure, he had engaged in his share of fisticuffs at the local bar, had swung on quite a few people that had insulted his wife. He had taken his share of bumps and bruises in return, even been knocked unconscious a few times, maybe more than a few. His cousin Junior had once told him he had a glass jaw. For the rest of that evening he imagined how cool it would be to actually have a jaw made out of glass. *What color would you make it? Would it be see-through?*

Despite all these bouts of violence, he had never tried to kill anyone, had never tried to make someone end. But here, in this world, it seemed to be a common occurrence.

The news, the ever-present news, droned on and on wherever he went. It seemed the people of this world were addicted to news, and it was never anything good. It was just a bunch of talking heads flapping and jawing, arguing and arguing, and the only thing they seemed to sow was fear—fear of others, fear of people who didn't believe the same tenets as the hosts.

The result of this, as far as Bud could see, was a steady parade of atrocities. Day after day, hour after hour, it seemed as if humanity was killing itself. One hour, some asshole would walk into a theater and shoot it up. Another hour, some twisted fuck would step into a school and shoot that up, and the talking heads would repeat the same catchphrases over and over. *Tragedy, hoax, false flag.*

It got so bad that the government, much to Bud's bemusement, passed the Fifty-second Amendment. He must have missed the Fifty-first in one of his brain blips. The Fifty-second Amendment was a frightening proposition indeed. It expanded upon the Second Amendment and said that not only did Americans have the right to bear arms, but that everyone, in an effort to achieve peace, had a responsibility to bear arms, and that those who refused would be shipped off to third-world countries because they were anti-American. This was the Patriot Party's grand solution.

From then on, the news was a parade of murders, mass shooting after mass shooting, and no one in the government seemed to care. No one wanted to do anything because of a line on a piece of parchment written hundreds of years ago by a bunch of slave-holding aristocrats. After a while, the news stopped seeming like news and more like a scoresheet where the lives of those lost were tallied up.

Despite the fact that America was packing heat, this heat didn't make anyone safer. Kids killed brothers and sisters. Parents killed kids. Police shot anything that moved. Even firefighters got into the action killing people burning alive in their flaming homes rather than risk their own lives to save them.

Rather than experience the nonstop barrage of violence, Bud turned within himself, only coming out of his shell every now and then to see if the world had improved. It never did.

****

On one such occasion, Bud found himself standing on a dais, overlooking an audience of humanity that he didn't even recognize. Their eyes were glazed and hard. Reporters, big and bulky, crammed into clothing that didn't seem to fit their bodies, milled around the room waiting.

One reporter bumped into another, and the offended man pulled a gun out and shot the first reporter in the back. The injured reporter, not dead yet, spun and pulled his own handgun from inside his jacket. He let loose with a flurry of fire that didn't come close to killing his original attacker. Bullets sprayed about the conference room, hitting some in the arm, some in the chest, and for one unfortunate soul, right in the forehead.

Bud had never quite found the trick to closing his eyes as a disembodied consciousness, and he witnessed all of the graphic carnage, though he wished he hadn't. From there, the room full of reporters opened fire on everyone. Bullets stitched Bud's corporeal form, and he felt the pain somewhere in the back of his mind, but only as an abstraction, a fact that meant nothing.

Policemen rushed into the room in full riot gear, and they finished the job the reporters had started. When everyone was still and the shooting stopped, machines whirred into the room and dragged the bodies away—a common sight these days. The days of a coroner going to each death were long gone. There simply weren't enough of them to keep up with the onslaught of murdered bodies. The robots bustled around the room on Inspector Gadget legs, stepping gingerly over corpses and snapping photos of the crime scene, while in one corner of the room the cops posed for pictures on their cell phones, their rifles pointing triumphantly at the sky.

Bud would have cried if he could. He had never seen humanity so inhumane.

When the robots had finished cataloguing the crime scene, they stood over each body, sucking them up into their hollow interiors the way Bud had imagined UFOs had abducted humans ripe for probing. They walked from the room on their metallic, rubber band legs, and the police high fived each other and disappeared, off to deliver another round of justice in another part of the city.

It was then the ceremony began amidst spent brass cartridges and bloodstains.

A man walked in, clean-cut, healthy in the way that only money could provide. His skin was clear, his hair perfectly maintained, and his suit was impeccably tailored. He was the commissioner of the Murderleague.

He walked across the stage and inspected the trophy, in this case, Bud.

With a leering smile, the commissioner whispered in Bud's ear, "Looks like you've seen better days, my old friend. But that's ok. This was gonna be your last rodeo anyway. Not enough room for names on you anymore, and no team wants to be engraved on your taint."

None of what the man said made sense to Bud; he was still trying to get over the disgusting carnage etched in his mind.

"You're going to the Hall of Fame, pal."

From there, the ceremony proceeded as usual. The winning team, The Fucks, came in. They showered the room with champagne and the hall filled with the smell of marijuana smoke which had been made legal sometime in the past. Bud guessed he had missed that update. Maybe it was like Amendment Forty-one or something.

The Fucks picked his body up and tossed it from member to member, lifting him in the air and braying like animals. The commissioner flashed golden teeth at the display, his beringed fingers flashing as he applauded the debauchery of The Fucks. Cameras, propelled by unseen propulsion systems, hovered about the room like flying saucers, flying this way and that, recording every conceivable angle as the roided-out athletes screamed like cavemen. Bud noticed they were covered from head to toe in tattoos just as he had been... but at least their markings had been a choice. Bud had no say in the matter;

his skin glistened in the blinding light of the cameras, names like Cody, Colt, Gunner, Trigger, and M4chin3 were scrawled all over his skin.

When the athletes began vomiting on stage, much to the delight of the commissioner, Bud's time ended as the original trophy of the Murderleague. His body was vacuum-packed and sent off to a museum, a place where all the iconic items of the Murderleague were given a place on podiums to be revered by the fans of the Murderleague's proud history.

For the next hundred years, he stood on a podium staring at beaming, fat faces with missing teeth and sores on their skin. They would come and stand in front of him, their backs to him as their own personal flying saucers snapped picture after picture. Then they would leave to go onto the next exhibit, a collection of early personalized controllers from the Murderleague's early days.

It was a peaceful time, the times that he could remember, at least.

CHAPTER 6: FÉLON DUSK AND DINGLECOINS

AS TIME PASSED, BUD became increasingly more detached from his body. He began to suspect that his spirit was like the air filling a Mylar balloon, and when his crotch had been broken off, his spirit had started to leak out ever so slowly. To Bud, this offered hope. He hoped for release every second of every day.

His wandering mind dreamed of seeing his loves; either of them or both, it didn't matter. He would be happy either way. When he wasn't dreaming of them, philosophy waylaid his mind, and he frequently found himself wondering if the next life was the last life, or if there were other worlds beyond the next. For the billionth time, he cursed himself and his stupid plan.

What if, by the time I make it to the next world, they've already moved onto the one after that? During these times, he would get down on himself, cursing himself for being an idiot. At times, he would rattle the bars of his cage, pummeling them with his mind, though this had no physical effect. *Why hadn't the church warned him of this?*

Though he had attended his fair share of church services with Barb, he had no recollection in his spotty mind of any priest ever saying that once you died, you would be trapped in your body. *Is this how it was for those thrown into graves? Were they all trapped underground in their coffins, sealed away from the air, cursed to wonder nonstop about the state of their loved ones in an ornate box?* If so, Bud considered himself lucky. At least his eternity hadn't been one of nonstop drudgery. Oh, there was plenty of drudgery, but at least he'd had a few breaks every now and then. The idea of staring at a coffin lid for the rest of eternity held no appeal for him. In that respect, he had been lucky.

But not as lucky as those that had chosen cremation, freed from their bodies and allowed to go onto the next world. He hoped Barb and his no-name Mexican lover had both chosen cremation, though it meant he might miss them in the next world.

It was during one of his more existential musings that something new happened, the first new thing in a hundred years or more by his recollection, although he could hardly rely on his own memory anymore.

The museum, once bustling and busy, had fallen into deep disrepair. The ever-bulbs had begun to fade somewhat, and in the dim illumination they gave off, a pair of shuffling weirdoes trundled along, hunched over and clad in rags.

They shattered the dusty glass around him and pulled him out of his display. When they spoke, they spoke in a language that he did not understand. But that was ok. He had the ability to acquire language now. Given enough time, he could puzzle out whatever language it was they were speaking.

They wrapped his body in an ancient sheet, olive green underneath all of the stains, and they dragged him through the city streets. A gust of hot wind blew the sheet off his head, though it still remained wrapped around his body.

He admired the buildings, tall and shiny. They looked like something out of a sci-fi movie. They gleamed and sparkled unlike any buildings he had ever seen before, jutting into the air like wolf teeth. Along the sides of the buildings, ads played, giant gaudy billboards, advertising items that made no sense to Bud. The letters on the ads looked strange to him, like English, but combined with other types of letters... maybe one of those Middle Eastern languages with all their swoops and swirls.

Down below, on the street level, things were drastically different. The streets were abandoned, empty, left to rot and ruin. Rats and creatures, vaguely human, scuttled through the streets. Everywhere, there were bullet holes.

On one charred brick wall, he spotted some graffiti that he could actually read. "R.I.P. Amercia." *Is being a bad speller a prerequisite to being a graffiti artist?* He wondered if the tag was just wishful thinking or fact, but there were no more answers hidden in the dilapidated streets.

The avenues and alleyways continued to pass, and nowhere did he see any sign of green. He had been longing for nature for the last twenty years, longing to see blue sky, a fucking tree in the wind. Hell, even a houseplant would have done it for him. He had never been a nature-lover like his cousin Marisa. She had been a water bug from day one, loved to kayak down the Rogue when they were kids, loved to get away from her family. At age seventeen, she had died in a drunken kayak accident. It was a shame. Out of all his cousins, he thought she could have been something. She might have been the smartest of his cousins, the smartest in his entire extended family. But hey, maybe that's why she had gone out on the river drunk in the first place. Imagine all of the pain she had avoided by dying. The young die pure, not twisted and weird.

Above him, in the sky, a line of fireflies moved among the tall, gleaming buildings, and then he figured out they were vehicles. All the cars he recognized lay on rusted rims, their windows busted in. They would never run again, and he wondered just how far into time he had traveled. *How much time has my kinked-up mind lost?*

After being dragged for hours, or minutes—Bud had no way of knowing—they descended into a deep, dank cellar.

They carried him gently and reverently down the stairs before setting him in a corner.

In their dank cellar, he watched them fuck each other. Their bodies dripped sweat, and their genitals didn't match up with what he had been expecting, but their coupling lit something in him, and he smiled at their care for each other. It had been so long since he had seen genuine love.

When they were done, they drank brown water from a spigot set in the wall, and they held each other tenderly, whispering in their strange language. At one point, the woman that was really a man began to cry and the man that was really a woman held the other. The faded ever-light in the ceiling glowed dimly, and they fell asleep holding each other. It was beautiful, and if he had been capable of crying, he would have. Though these people were nothing like him, it was the only act of kindness he had seen in quite some time, and it moved him, made him feel like everything was going to be alright.

In the morning, they ate a breakfast of moss and mushrooms picked lovingly off the corpse rotting in the corner of the room. Then they bundled Bud up in a musty sheet and dragged him through the city streets in a harsh daylight that made him wish he could sweat. The world was hot, and harsh dust blew in the spaces between buildings. A ragged, drying wind whipped about the cloaks of the lovers as they trundled through the city.

Above, the vehicles had disappeared, and the gleaming skyscrapers were sealed with steel shutters to block out the cooking sun. The lovers avoided spots of bright sunshine like children playing a game of hot lava. When they came to a patch of sun they couldn't avoid, they sprinted through it, and into the shadows. Once in the shadows, they would peel off their cloaks and stand naked in the street, their cloaks steaming upon the ground and sweat running down their bodies. When the cloaks cooled, they would don them once again and continue their trek.

They traveled like this for days, and then they came to the bottom of one of the giant skyscrapers. It hovered above them, jets of bright-blue flame holding the skyscraper in the sky. They dragged him under the flames, and the building's base blotted out the sky. In his mind, he imagined those bright blue flames going out and the skyscraper crashing down upon him, trapping him in his taxidermied body forever.

But the flames held, and from above, within the square of the skyscraper's bottom, a light flared a hundred feet in the sky, highlighting the lovers and their cargo. In the light, Bud could see that the skin of his body had darkened where the sun had kissed him.

A ship, small and capable of carrying only one or two people, detached from the skyscraper. It corkscrewed down to the surface of the earth in a long spiraling descent, and then, it landed. Two women stepped out— healthy-looking, vibrant, like the humans of his youth. In their hands they waved wands, metallic and shiny in the direction of the lovers.

They spoke in their strange language, and the uniformed women spoke back, their handle of the language harsh and guttural. One of the women stepped to the back of the flying vehicle and pulled out a white leather bag with a red cross emblazoned on the side. She tossed the bag at the two lovers, and the woman who was really a man caught it in her hands, squeezing it tight like it was going to fly away at any moment.

The two lovers bowed gently at the two uniformed women. In response, the women aimed their weapons threateningly at the couple. The lovers retreated slowly and reverently, backing away from the skyscraper. The woman who was really a man held a death grip on the bag, and when they were far enough away, they turned and ran from the uniformed women. Bud wished them well.

Then, the two women stuffed him in the back of their flying car, and he took a winding ride up into the skyscraper.

As the car docked, Bud couldn't help but be awed by the difference within the skyscraper. Here, people looked healthy, everything was bright, lit by ever-lights that simulated daylight, rich and warm. It wasn't real nature, but Bud liked it better than the actual sunshine that had cooked the skin of his body.

When the vehicle landed, the two women stood still while another man blasted them with a foggy concoction from the end of something that looked quite like a fire extinguisher. When this was done, the man set the fire extinguisher aside and ran a gloved hand over their bodies. The glove beeped and whirred as machinery inside scanned the women. The fingers of the glove flashed green, and the two women, their test passed, placed Bud on a floating platform.

Floating as if in a dream, Bud beheld the wonderland of the future. Everywhere he looked he saw things which made no sense to him. The people were tall and of all colors. They looked healthy, unlike the poor, hunched creatures who dwelled on the surface of the Earth. The uniformed women strode confidently through the shining, white streets of the skyscraper, which was more massive than anything he could have ever imagined.

As a boy, he remembered staring up at a tree as his Uncle Brandon had rested underneath, eating an apple, one arm behind his head and one leg resting over the top of the other, his boot dangling in the air. The old oak tree rose into the sky, a work of art made by nature. The leaves on the tree glowed a bright orange. As he stared up at those lofty heights, secret acorns dropped around him to land unseen into the dry leaves. Tilting his head back, he would stare at the top of the massive tree until his head began to swim. Then, a leaf would fall, and he would rush after it, running through the open field where Uncle Brandon worked as a field hand. Clomping over uneven thickets of grass and fallen branches, he would run and run, chasing down the leaves that plummeted from the top of the tree, rushing up underneath them to catch the dying leaf in his hands. Once he grasped its fragile dying form, he would hold it to his nose and breathe in its scent. On this Earth, which no longer made sense to him, he didn't imagine there would ever be another kid who would experience such simple joy.

As his mind wandered, two sliding doors shushed open, and he was pushed into an elevator. Up and up they went, the numbers on the elevator's panel reaching triple digits, and then reaching quadruple digits. At floor number 1368, the elevator chimed, and the doors slid open. His escorts pushed him into a great open space. If Bud could have moved his jaw, it would have dropped open.

On this floor, the skyscraper had ceased to be the inside of a building. All around him, trees grew, moss clinging to their trunks. Somewhere in this natural space, water trickled. Grass swayed in a manufactured breeze, and he could see the tiny specks of insects as they flitted about the forest.

A human stood in front of him, with a smile on his face. Whoever he was, he was simply human, and Bud was overjoyed to be in his presence, removed from the dingy prison of the Murderleague Hall of Fame.

Though he grinned a pawnbroker's grin, the smile never touched his eyes. This man clapped his hands together, overjoyed. "You found him!" the being said. The two women nodded and propelled Bud toward the man. "Did you have any problem with the dregs?"

"No," one of the women said, "they seemed to appreciate the cancer meds. I don't know how they survive down there, nasty little things."

"Now, Mursula. Remember, they are us. If I left you down there, you would look just like one of them in no time."

"I doubt it. I'd sooner hang myself."

The man's smile disappeared. "You know the rule against negative talk."

"I'm sorry, Félon."

"I accept your apology. Please report to the generator room to pay your penance."

The women bowed deeply, and then both the women left, leaving Bud alone with the man.

His face was wide, his eyes seemed half dead, and he smiled in the queerest way at Bud. He didn't fully trust the smile, as it had something about the coyote about it. He had seen that smile before. His great uncle, a violent drunk had always smiled like that before he was going to lay into you. He had attacked a cop once with that smile on his face, and that was the last they saw of him, until the funeral.

"Bud, Bud, Bud." Félon stepped up to Bud and placed his hands on his plaster shoulders. His hands were smooth, soft, free of the damage a life of hard work can do to a man. Félon was soft, worthless in every way, and Bud could sense it.

"I'm so happy to have you here. I know Murderleague is a thing of the past, but I've seen every match. I scoured the ancient-net for years, pulling hidden plugs of data and matches out of the past, resurrecting them for my own viewing. Oh, sure, it's highly illegal to own any footage of Murderleague. Most of the Global Council wants to pretend like it didn't even happen, but not me. No, I love the savagery, the go-for-broke desperation of those old gamers. So, when I discovered the location of the old Hall of Fame... I just had to send someone to look. And they found you!" Félon tapped Bud on the nose with a small, "Boop!" Then he smiled that toothy, coyote-ish grin.

"You are my prize possession."

Félon spoke a word that Bud failed to recognize, and a chair thrust itself out of the ground. With a happy sigh, Félon sat on it and leaned back as the chair whirred, massaging the man's back. For hours, that's the way they sat. Félon studying Bud, and Bud studying him right back.

Eventually, Bud tired of studying the strange man. He made him feel uncomfortable in a way that he had never felt before. There was something wrong with the man, something off. In him, he sensed an incompleteness, a lack of the spark that made a person a human.

"I know all about you, Bud. I know you killed yourself in the summer of 1985. I know that your wife kept you at your house for twenty years after that, and then, one Hector Montalban purchased you and brought you to his whorehouse, The Donkey Club, in Juarez, Mexico. It was then that you were found by the inaugural champions of Murderleague." The man read these facts to Bud emotionlessly, as if he were but a robot, programmed to recite information. "That was the most brutal year. The prize was big enough to bring out all the heavy hitters. Oh, the matches were amazing, no rules, no protections against hacks, no glitch penalties. No limits. Just one team destroying another. That team could kill like nobody else. Their championship win, the one that sealed the deal was one of the most stunning wins of all-time, not because it was unexpected, but because of the way they did it. There they were, the two-teams' captains deep in a one-v-one of Soldier Simulator 2120, and Beef Ramsey—he would be a hall of famer too—snuck up on M3di4tor, proceeds to tea-bag behind the ignorant fool, and then killed him with two punches to the back of the head. How about that? This man, M3di4tor, had trained for years, and then he's teabagged and knocked out like a five-year-old just picking up a controller. That was it for old M3di4tor. His chair circuits fired and fried him right on the spot." Félon made a sizzling sound and jerked around as if being electrocuted. "It was the best season ever. Over two hundred competitors, none sure what they were getting themselves into, only that they would be rich as hell at the end of it all—if they won."

Félon smiled at Bud, a fire in his eyes. "But like any true stroke of genius, the dumb dumbs had to come along and water it down. Make it safe. They did it in the twentieth century with things like seatbelts and warnings on everything. They took everything fun and dangerous and made it kid friendly, and that was the start of the end."

Félon stood then, his chair disappearing into the floor. Wrapping a soft hand around Bud's bicep, he dragged Bud's floating platform through the resplendent natural setting. As Félon rambled on and on about Murderleague, and its ever-softening rule changes, Bud took deep breaths of the air, breathing in the smell of earth, the smell of trees. By God, he could actually smell the tree bark.

Eventually, the nature fell away, and he found himself in a room like something from an old sci-fi movie. It was clean, empty, white. He hated it. A gleaming steel desk sat in the middle of the room, a screen set into its width. Behind the desk, he saw the most glorious sight, the world from the top of the skyscraper. As far as he could tell, he was in the tallest one. The tops of the other skyscrapers hovered below, thick clouds wrapping around their spires, and the glare from the sun would have blinded him if he were in his mortal body.

Félon, still rambling about Murderleague, guided Bud's body to a glass case and shoved him inside. A brief hum and a flash of blue clued Bud into the fact that he was now sealed inside the case, though as Felon continued to ramble, he found the forcefield protecting him did not block out sound. *That's too bad.*

"Anyway, I'm glad you're here." Félon scanned the spartan office, its harsh lines and clean surfaces. "It gets lonely at the top."

Then he went to his desk and sat down. He waved his hand over the screen in his desk, and a translucent image flared into life, hanging in the air. Félon, his hands a whirlwind of activity, gestured at the hologram with his hands, and every time he did, somewhere, someone smaller than him had their life irrevocably changed. For the better or for the worse, it didn't matter to Félon.

And this is how life went on, brief diatribes from Félon and long periods of watching him wave his hands in the air. Sometimes, Bud would inch out of his crotch hole and turn around and watch the world behind him, a sky of limitless potential, skyscrapers dwarfed beneath its immensity. It was really more interesting than Félon's ramblings. For as powerful a man as he was, he was quite boring.

****

Bud watched a vaguely human cloud rip apart in the sky, its middle thinned and then shredded. The wind carried the two halves apart. It reminded him of his father, a simple man who had worked in factories his entire life. He had toiled with his hands, worked to provide for his family, though he had nothing more than an Indian public school education and a lot of pent-up rage to show for it. It only stood that at the end of a long work week, he would go out for a drink and blow off some steam. Sometimes he blew off too much steam and left himself deflated. One such night, his deflated body passed out in the road. A semi-truck had come along and broke his body in half... much like that cloud. They had cremated him rather than have a burial. One of his cousins, an older boy named Ricky, had told him that when the truck ran over him, his guts, organs, and other things had sprayed out of both ends, and this was why they hadn't had an open casket.

He envied his father, not his death— that had been hard. But he did envy how quickly he had escaped his body. Cremation... cremation. If he had it to do over again, he would have been cremated, turned into hundreds of pounds of ash and dust and energy. He would have had his body spread on the Rogue River, the home of his ancestors and their ancestors before them. His body, separated, sprinkled, and cast to the wind would have been free, flowing all over the Earth. He imagined it would be like having cable, and enough TVs to play every channel all at once. Except for the news ones. He had watched enough news in his life... most of it bad.

"You know, Bud. Some people think it would be really fun to be in charge of the world. Not me. I find it... rather tedious. I mean, once you become the most powerful, richest man in the world, what the hell are you supposed to do then?"

Félon leaned back in his chair, the massage motors whirring and kneading his back.

"I've reached all of my goals, and sometimes I feel like a giant, looking down on an anthill. In this metaphor, the entirety of humanity is the anthill. You get it, Bud? How can I not play with them, for they are all that I have? They are the reason I am in this position. Watch this."

Félon pressed a button of skin on his wrist, and a face appeared in hologram form, hovering in front of him. "Lester, I'd like you to sell two-hundred-thousand shares of DingleCoin. Shortly after that, oh, let's say by noon, I'd like you to zwipzwap the following to my millions of followers: Dusk Industries is no longer interested in trading DingleCoin. Instead, we are unrolling today a form of currency backed by Dusk Industries. We call them DuskBucks, and they allow you to own a piece of Dusk Industries."

"Sir, uh, what are DuskBucks?"

"I don't know, Lester. I just made them up. Anyways, zwipzwap that to my followers, make some DuskBucks, and we'll be rolling in billions by teatime."

Lester, in a very serious voice said, "What time is teatime?"

"I don't know, Lester. It's an old expression."

"Right."

Félon pressed the button on his wrist, and the interface disappeared once again, leaving Bud and Félon alone in his office.

"Did you see that, Bud?" Félon stood from his chair, stretching his back. "Do you know what I just did there? I crushed the fortunes of a thousand people who believed in me, believed that on some level I had their best interests in mind. Now, they're panicking, looking to sell their shares of DingleCoin as fast as they can. And you know what I'm going to do after that? I'm going to snap up all that DingleCoin at an even lower price. I'll zwipzwap some bullshit about how I made a tactical error, and then the price of my money will go through the roof. Why? Because money is bullshit. Money, stocks, currency... it's all made up. If you can convince people that you have power, then you actually have power. These poor bastards don't get that. All they see is numbers..."

Bud went back to watching the clouds in the sky. Over the years, he had learned that Félon Dusk was nothing more than the shell of a man. All the money in the world, all the power, and he did nothing with it but push it around like an ape playing with his own shit. What was the point?

He had never had much, but his life had been happier than this monstrous dipshit before him, yammering about stocks, options, double-tanks, and zwipzwap, whatever the hell that was. It took a monster to make money, and that was a fact, as true as the faded names tattooed upon his chest.

Despite the losses of his family, year after year, despite the loss of his own mind, he had never been a monster. He had lived a life he was proud of, up until that fateful day that he had shot his brains through the back of his skull. Still, he'd rather live an eternity trapped in his body rather than one week in the body of Félon Dusk. There was never a bigger, falser, nuttier turd in the world than Félon Dusk. He was an idiot savant of sorts. Instead of seeing people and corporations, and lives, and sons and daughters, and pets... he saw numbers to move around, Add, subtract, split dividends. It was all a game to him. If he was the best humanity had to offer, then he would be grateful when humanity was dead and gone.

"You want to see true power, Bud? It's coming. You just wait and see. Soon, I will make a decision that will affect every man woman and child. It's going to be glorious!"

Bud ignored the man, didn't give two crotch holes how he was going to make money. The numbers Félon threw around made no sense to him. He didn't even know how much money a quadrillion was, couldn't conceive of it, and therefore, didn't care.

Swirling among an electrical storm, he watched the clouds. Flashes of light, sharp and bright, were worth more than however many DingleBucks Félon had in his imaginary wallet.

****

Over time, Félon Dusk's malaise became all encompassing. He grew bored with life and obsessed with death. As his body wrinkled, and his wife passed away, he turned in upon himself. Félon's one contribution to the planet came in the form of a child that everyone called Einstein. Einstein's proud parents had written $E=MC^2$ on his birth certificate, a pretentious, ostentatious, and thoroughly droll publicity stunt. In reality, everyone just called the kid Einstein, and he was as terrible a child as one could expect.

Félon, now wrinkled and old, his face deformed from youth-enhancing procedures, couldn't stand the bastard, though he was essentially a chip off the old block. With his own mortality facing him, Félon had become obsessed with death, the way that Bud had right before his own unfortunate demise. Bud had chosen his way out, and it seemed as if Felon was on the same path.

"You know, Bud. It's a shame really. I thought Einstein would be my legacy. I thought he would carry on my name and my company, but he seems disinterested in the business. It seems I am doomed to disappear."

Dusk walked with a hovercane now. Without it, he hobbled around the room like Bud's second cousin Walter, who had broken his leg while riding a bronco when they were younger. Just like that, Walter's rodeo career was over. In that single moment, Walter's entire life disappeared, though it would take him years to find out. After the injury, he had gotten involved in the church and its youth group. It came as a big surprise when they found him hanging from a rope around his neck in one of the back rooms.

As if appearing out thin air, the wrinkled, aged, and pointless visage of Félon obscured Bud's view. He could smell the death on his breath. The man was on his way out, and that likely meant old Einstein would be taking ownership of Bud... and that likely meant an eternity in storage somewhere.

"You know, Bud. If I can't live forever, then I don't think it's fair that anyone else can."

Félon shook his head and hobbled around the room. He tapped the button on his wrist and a face appeared in hologram form in front of him. "Mattice, I want to initiate Project Eraser."

"Are you sure, sir?" Mattice asked as a pained look crossed his face.

"Have you ever known me to be unsure?"

"No, sir."

Bud didn't think anything of the conversation, but very soon he would.

****

He was staring out of Dusk's window at two clouds that looked like gymnasts in mid-tumble when a couple of burly men with growths all over their face appeared. They smelled musky and dank, as if their clothes hadn't been washed in months, and truthfully, that was the case. Water was too rare and too expensive for a common worker to afford to wash their clothes.

They hunched into Félon Dusk's office, lowered the forcefield on Bud's case, and floated him out and through a brown, dead forest. He never even got the chance to say goodbye.

On his short trip from the elevator, he took in the sights. People huddled in corners. The stench coming off their bodies filled the empty spaces with gag-worthy aromas. Every stretch of bare skin seemed to be covered in black growths and nodules, and they coughed and hacked up blood. The workers that carried him ignored the poor bastards. Around him, he saw signs that the perfect world within the skyscraper was crumbling. The walls were plastered with graffiti, brown and scatish. The people kept their heads down, lest they confront their own fate. The lights that had glared so bright upon his entry into the skyscraper, blinked and strobed as if their circuits were on their last legs. The halls were humid and over-hot, reeking of death and rot. A man, his arm covered in black nodules fell to the ground, gasping for air. The workers pushed right past him, winding him through the halls of the skyscraper where the scenery never changed.

Soon, he found himself loaded into a conical space filled with buttons and glowing lights. They secured his body with buckles and straps, and he examined his new home. The walls were made of a clear material, too clear to be glass, and he seemed to be perched atop the very same skyscraper that he had lived in for a lifetime. The clouds were wonderful today, dark and stormy, and heavy with moisture, just the way he liked them.

"Have a nice trip, Bud!" one of the workers said, and then they sealed the door to his new home. Maybe old Félon had finally died, passed away, and this was to be his final resting place. He wondered how long it would be until he was forgotten completely.

Somewhere in the basement of the skyscraper, Dusk's men toiled away working on a project that would spell their own doom. But hey, the pay was good, so how could they deny it? Though there was a countdown in the bowels of the skyscraper, Bud heard none of it. One minute, he was sitting in his conical pod, and the next he was rocketing through the atmosphere.

The whole affair reminded him of being on a rollercoaster. His body pressed into the seat as gravity quickened, and then he was lifting to the sky, heading to the black of outer space. On a screen, he watched as the base of a giant monolith, Dusk's skyscraper he supposed, flared bright white, a cloud of white exhaust rocking and shaking the cameras. The skyscraper lifted into the air, and Bud understood that he was leaving the planet.

Up and up they went, the massive skyscraper climbing higher and higher. The air became thin around the see-through, conical prison, and Bud could see the heat and flames of friction licking the translucent walls.

And then came the explosion, like a trillion Black Cats going off at once. The floor of the cone shook underneath him as rockets roared to life. His pod separated from the skyscraper. The screen stopped showing the skyscraper from below, and switched to a vision of the skyscraper from above, very likely from a camera mounted on the bottom of Bud's own personal spaceship.

The heat and the flames vanished, and he took in a grand picture of the moon as he shot by its cratered face. The surface of the moon was littered with junk, abandoned rovers, golf balls, a Dusk Industries rocket poking out of a crater, and a massive billboard for Murderleague. It looked like a white trash front yard. All that was missing was a discarded toilet and a junked-out Ford pickup truck.

He was so enthralled he almost missed the view from the screen. Below him, rockets on the top of the skyscraper fired, driving the skyscraper downward, plunging it like a giant dagger into the Earth's heart. Even in the void of space, he felt the shockwave of his planet's death, fomented by unchecked power and made-up currency. It was the end of Earth, and Bud felt nothing. It seemed to him that Earth had died long ago, and these were just its death throes.

The skyscraper plunged into the earth, hitting with the mass and force of a giant asteroid. Dusk's words rang in his ears. "If I can't live forever, then no one can." Say goodbye humanity. It probably came a little too late to be honest. The only thing he really felt bad for were all the animals and plants. They didn't deserve to die along with humanity, but they would rise again he suspected. Maybe the next time, the apex lifeform wouldn't be such destructive dicks.

Dusty, gritty clouds obscured the blue of Earth's oceans. The planet's lights, dotting the world like a virus, disappeared under the bruise-like clouds.

Good, Bud thought. He hoped the spirits of his ancestors had all been released from their coffin tombs, that they could fly free and enjoy the sanctity of not being.

CHAPTER 7: THE LONG DARK

IT SEEMED AS IF, ever since Bud had been a child, he had dreamed of going to space. It was the last frontier, the last place where a person could be completely free. Now that he had made it to space, he found himself absolutely bored. There was nothing out here, only him in his stupid pod, his body, and his rambling, wandering mind.

He had begun to fracture, turn into two beings, one who lived constantly in the past, and another lesser being who sat and drooled at the darkness around him like a shut-in watching recorded Wheel of Fortune re-runs on their VCR. That being stared at the cold blackness of space, its eyes searching the pinprick dotted void, for something, anything that would break up the monotony. Light years, that's what that being was in the saddle for, absolute light years of silence and observance.

This being, the Saddle Man the other being called it, began to feel as if he was in Hell, a vast emptiness where nothing changed, nothing was ever different. Did those pinpricks of light come closer with every second he shuttled through space? If they did, Saddle Man could not tell.

The other being, Bud, went on all sorts of adventures, trapped in his own failing mind. He visited the past every day, replaying the world until his memories became warped. His wife, Barb, now had brown skin and spoke with a Mexican accent. In other memories, his no-name lover rode him and rode him, her shiny face glowing in the red light of the whorehouse in Félon Dusk's modern office, the stub of a cigar chomped between her brown teeth.

In some of those memories, he was still alive, still capable of walking. He relived the moment of his death over and over again, replaying his suicide... only, the details were fuzzy now. Sometimes he shot himself, sometimes he ate a spoonful of rat poison. Sometimes the taxidermist—he had forgotten his name—choked the life out of him as a favor.

The essence of Bud splintered and fractured, and he found himself having conversations with the different aspects of himself.

This is Hell, twenty-year-old Bud said.

A drunk Bud, from his wedding night, said, *You think this is hell. I don't think I'll be able to get it up tonight. Beer dick.*

Twenty-year-old Bud scoffed at drunk Bud. *Getting married is for suckers. I'm going to be single for the rest of my life.*

Not after you find that special girl.

All girls are special.

A small voice crept in, child Bud, damaged and scared. *It's too dark out here. Someone turn on the lights.*

Go to sleep, baby boy. This is adult business, said the twenty-year-old version of himself.

****

While the versions of Bud argued among themselves and tried to pin down the verisimilitude of Bud's memories, Saddle Man watched the universe slip by in a never-ending, never-blinking gaze. As he did, time began to slip, and as one moment became the next became the next, they contracted into one single moment. Bound by the eye of the beholder, in this case Saddle Man, time became a kaleidoscope of shifting stars, galaxies and darkness, twisting and turning until it seemed to freeze and stop altogether.

What had been a light year, was nothing more than a second. What had been infinity became a short scream. Saddle Man sailed past stars and planets of all shapes and sizes. The ones with the rings were the best. His pod shot by pulsing stars that should have burned him alive and sucked him into their gravitational pull, freeing Saddle Man from existing at all. But somehow, he threaded his way through galaxies, spinning spirals of gas and rock, like a trick-shot arrow.

One day, a small spaceship arrived, and Saddle Man stared at the faces of alien beings looking through a small porthole as they matched the speed of his pod. Inside, one of the diamond-headed, rubbery creatures stared at him for a bit, made an unflattering face, placed the middle of its nine fingers against the porthole, and then sped off.

Saddle Man, despite just being cursed by an intergalactic lifeform, felt nothing, and the pod wended its way through time and space as the real Bud devolved into a thousand different versions of himself... each one living in their own hell. Together, they screamed at each other, cursing and accusing, though they were all the same, just different points on a lifeline. Every problem they had was infinitesimally small and infinitely all-encompassing. This was how they stayed sane in the void.

CHAPTER 8: THE NEW GOD, JUST AS POINTLESS AS THE FIRST

BUD COULDN'T SAY HOW long the journey lasted, but eventually, after passing through asteroid belts, skirting entire galaxies, and floating through all manner of starlight, his body, now irradiated beyond measure, dried out and twisted, made its way to a planet. The million different versions of himself collapsed upon themselves like the controlled demolition of a skyscraper, floor after floor collapsing onto the next, leaving a giant cloud of dust in its wake. The rubble left behind was named Bud. He found himself again, whole, wholly confused, and once again back in the saddle of the Saddle Man. For the first time since he had been visited by aliens, there was something to do other than cannibalize his own consciousness to retain a spark of the man that he once was.

The planet shone pink and blue. The star that lit its surface glowed a shining emerald, and his vision, not the vision of his corporeal eyes, but of his consciousness, grew accustomed to its glittery luminescence. His space pod penetrated the planet's atmosphere gently, and he floated through the sky of a new world. The gravity was not strong enough to bring his pod down, and he became a part of the skyscape.

He dubbed the world Watermelon because the pink earth reminded him of the flesh of the watermelons his grandmother had grown in her garden. Below, he could see seeds, writhing among the flesh. The seeds were the population of the planet, primitive and simple. Bud enjoyed watching them. From his vantage point, they were like his own personal ant farm. As time slipped by, he circled the planet like a Thanksgiving Day float in a never-ending orbit in Watermelon's upper atmosphere, watching the creatures below. He began to think of them as pets.

****

Good things were never meant to last. There was no rule in the universe that was truer. His love for Barb, his life with her, had been doomed from the get-go, so much so there were times he wished he had never met her at the bar that fateful night. He wished he had appreciated his life while he had it, wished he had taken advantage of every moment. He knew he had been selfish at the end of his life. He had sacrificed what little time he had because it wouldn't be perfect; it wouldn't be what he was accustomed to. If he could go back in time, he would, and even though his memory would fade, and he would eventually shit his pants, he would still take those moments, relish them. He would take Barb's tears because she deserved them, and he deserved it as well. They didn't deserve anything else, not money, not riches, not little Buds and Bud-ettes running through a sprinkler... but they deserved to end it, to let it play out despite the pain of knowing it was all going to end on some random day with a load in Bud's drawers, drool on his lips, and tears in Barb's eyes.

As regret rattled around in his hollowed-out head, the inhabitants below took notice of their extraterrestrial visitor floating in the sky.

They wondered about him and his strange shape, so unlike their own. Over the years, as he tripped into memories and ponderings and shame, the creatures in the ant farm grew and evolved, until they could make things. The vibrant pink flesh of Watermelon became dotted with settlements as the creatures below adapted the environment to their needs and wants. They reproduced, dotting the earth with ugly cities like planetary melanomas.

Bud didn't know why, but this made him sad. It was better when they slept on the pink beaches and bathed in its blue waters.

Eventually, their buildings climbed taller and taller, reaching higher and higher as their technology advanced. Their creations were spindly things, soft and waving in the weak gravity of the planet. Sometimes, he would see one of the creatures jump from their building and plummet to his death. They had learned to hate themselves now. They had learned to defy life, and Bud knew this was the downfall of the ant farm, for once the people no longer wanted to live, they overwrote every instinct in their body and perverted it. Once this happened, the sickness spread.

Soon, the pink flesh of the planet turned brown and ugly. The air filled with smoggy clouds as factory after factory pumped out smoke and fire into the air.

One day, one of the skyscrapers reached as high as Bud's pod. One of the creatures, standing at the very apex of the building, reached out and brushed Bud's tomb with his hand. The look of wonder on the creature's face made him miserable. Sometime after that, they wrapped blue, fuzzy ropes around his tomb and pulled him to the ground. He was among them now, staked to the faded pink flesh of Watermelon, so he wouldn't float away.

He regarded their misshapen heads, flatter than he could have imagined a living creature's head could be. Their eyes bulged out of those flat heads, twitching on stalks, silver and pupilless.

They placed him in the center of one of their cities, and the ants came to visit him, bowing before him. Bud, gifted at language acquisition now, was quickly able to make out their words after a millennium or two. It turned out they worshipped him, called him God, and they made rules in his name, though Bud had no capability to utter such rules. This irked Bud for some reason.

An entire industry was built around copying his tattoos onto manufactured paper. They tore down their rainforests to make the paper and replicate his tattoos in books, whereupon a man in a brown suit with squiggly lines all over it, not unlike Bud's skin, would interpret the tattoos in the books for the masses.

Bud understood this was the beginning of religion on Watermelon, and that time would be short now.

If he had a heart in his chest, it would have broken then.

One day, one of the flathead people stormed into Bud's church and waved around a piece of paper. "You have interpreted the tattoos all wrong! They are just names!" the flathead yelled.

"Blasphemy!" the man in the suit yelled back. He was the hundredth man to wear the suit, give or take a few. And then, the flathead waving the paper shot the man in the suit with a green-rayed weapon. After, chaos reigned. They sacrificed themselves and murdered each other in Bud's name, over the interpretation of the tattoos on his body, and Bud felt terrible sorrow.

They're just names! He screamed in his mind. But no one stopped to listen. They had never wanted a God. They had simply wanted answers and a means of control, a means to hold back the wasting reality of life lived without purpose.

The wars intensified, and they stripped Watermelon's flesh to create newer and more destructive weapons. And then they blew it up. They blew up their entire planet, and Bud with it.

One minute, he was sobbing in his own mind at the atrocities committed in his name, and the next, there was a blinding flash of green light. For a second, the world transformed into an X-Ray version of itself. His tomb cracked and melted, and then his skin, the wood within, and the plaster of his fake body went up in glorious flames. He burned as bright as a sun for one whole second, and then he was gone. He was no more.

There was nothing after that. No Barb, no nameless Mexican gal, no shiny faced man, no Félon Dusk. There was absolutely nothing. And that's the way it was and will be.

ABOUT THE AUTHOR

JACY MORRIS is a Native American author born in 1979 in Virginia. He is a registered member of the Confederated Tribes of Siletz. At the age of ten he was transplanted to Portland, Oregon, where he developed a love for punk rock and horror movies, both of which tend to find their way into his writing. He has been an English and social studies teacher in Portland, Oregon since 2005.

He has written several books, including the "This Rotten World" series, *The Pied Piper of Hamelin*, *Killing the Cult*, and "The Enemies of Our Ancestors" series... and many more!

If you want to know more, check out jacymorris.com, his official website.

www.ingramcontent.com/pod-product-compliance
Lightning Source LLC
Chambersburg PA
CBHW020601130626
46552CB00007B/2992